T0095228

Realm of Power

Realm of Power

- INVASION -

JASON LEE ZIMMERMAN

REALM OF POWER
INVASION

iUniverse books may be ordered through booksellers or by contacting:

iUniverse
1663 Liberty Drive
Bloomington, IN 47403
www.iuniverse.com
1-800-Authors (1-800-288-4677)

Because of the dynamic nature of the Internet, any web addresses or
links contained in this book may have changed since publication and
may no longer be valid. The views expressed in this work are solely those
of the author and do not necessarily reflect the views of the publisher,
and the publisher hereby disclaims any responsibility for them.

Author Photo Credit: Jennie Schilling

Any people depicted in stock imagery provided by Thinkstock are models,
and such images are being used for illustrative purposes only.
Certain stock imagery © Thinkstock.

ISBN: 978-1-4917-7852-4 (sc)
ISBN: 978-1-4917-7851-7 (e)

Library of Congress Control Number: 2015919012

Print information available on the last page.

iUniverse rev. date: 11/16/2015

— CHAPTER ONE —

The Storm of Chaos

FOR YEARS WE HAVE ATTEMPTED TO CONTACT intelligent life other than our own, and for years they have remained silent. We should have guessed that there was a reason for the silence, but by that time it would have already been too late.

Washington DC was among the first casualties. Without any warning or explanation, the great city was wiped from the face of the earth in a matter of seconds. The president, secretary of defense, and joint chiefs, along with six hundred thousand inhabitants, were killed. Before anyone on the planet knew what was happening, Ottawa, Brasilia, and Buenos Aires suffered the same fate—within only minutes of each other.

Deep in the heart of the vast Australian outback, night had fallen. A small but diverse group of people had gathered. Some were rich, some were poor, and some were mothers clinging to their children as if they were afraid death had come for them all. There, one hope lay in the hands of an Australian shaman.

The Shaman was a dark-skinned man with a black beard and black hair. He wore a tunic around his pelvis, and a small sack hung around his neck. Oddly enough, he also wore a black leather jacket. Other than the jacket, this man looked as if he had lived out in the bush for years: The shaman sat Indian style in front of a campfire, which he stirred with a stick.

All waited anxiously to hear the shaman speak about their fate, yet he remained silent. A limousine pulled up to the campfire, and out stepped a very rich-looking man holding an ancient, ornate box. The shaman got up and walked over to the rich man, who handed him the box. As the shaman opened it, a strange, unearthly light shone out of it. Everyone, including the rich man, seemed to be filled with fear and dread at the sight of the light—except for the shaman.

The shaman slowly closed the box and turned to the people. "Brothers and sisters, I know why you are all here. The time of which I have spoken is at hand. For she has come, the angel of light with blood on her hands, to steal, kill, and destroy. Whether or not humanity can withstand her rage, I know not. Yet do not let your hearts be troubled, for the savior of all things will come and will fight by our sides to destroy the vile evil that she represents. But take heed: many will die, and many will rise before the end."

After looking at the box in his hands, he continued.

"For now we must hold out, but I promise I will do all in my power to keep this orb from her sight."

In China, General Vang Kai of the Chinese Red Guard was sleeping peacefully at his house on base in the city of Beijing. He was awakened by the telephone. "General, We have a code black! Repeat, we have a code black!"

General Vang Kai's eyes opened widely as he jumped up from his bed. He knew what this meant. Even though he had tried to prepare for all possibilities, he found himself completely unprepared. "Is the cloaking device still active?"

"Yes, General, but we don't know how effective it will be. Moscow has already been hit, as well as most of the capitals of North and South America."

"How long ago?" asked General Vang Kai.

"Moments, sir!"

General Vang Kai realized he was up against an enemy unlike any he had ever faced before. It was an enemy that could wipe out entire cities in a matter of minutes. Still, he knew his duty was to protect China—and also the only thing that he held most dear, his niece and only surviving relative, his brother's daughter.

General Vang Kai gave the order. "I want the orb moved immediately. We must get it to a more secure location!"

"Yes, General."

With that, General Vang Kai hung up the phone, put on his uniform as quickly as he could, and ran down to his eighteen-year-old niece's bedroom. Huiliang! Huiliang!" he said, trying desperately to wake her up.

She was still half-asleep and in her nightgown. "What is it, Uncle?"

"No time to explain!" he said, grabbing her bathrobe out of the closet. "Put this on. We need to go—now!"

General Vang Kai and Huiliang left the house accompanied by several Chinese soldiers. They made their way to several Chinese military vans parked on the side of the road in front of their house. Suddenly something appeared like a flash of lightning, and it struck the group of vans in front of them. The force of the blast threw General Vang Kai, Huiliang, and the Chinese soldiers backward. When they recovered, they looked up at the vans and could hardly believe their eyes.

There on top of the rubble of one of the vans stood the most beautiful being they had ever seen. She wore no garments, but then, she didn't need to. Her skin was more like a skintight jumpsuit over a flawless female frame. Her skin was whiter than snow. Beautiful white wings came out of her back, and a white tail came out of the bottom of her spinal column. Beautiful white feathers came out of the back of her legs and arms. Her fingernails were long with a brilliant shade of purple, like natural extensions. Her lips and hair were also purple. She seemed to have no pupils, but her eyes glowed with a brilliant purple light, as if a great and beautiful power lived within her. Her body as a whole gave off a beautiful white light. She was a divinely beautiful being before them and looked more like a goddess.

At first General Vang Kai and the rest of the soldiers thought that this beautiful being was there to help them, but that assumption quickly went away when they saw the type of company she kept. On her left side stood the most hideous monster that General Vang Kai had ever seen. His skin was a sickening shade of white—the type of white one expected to see on a deceased corpse. Two horns came out of the back of his head and curled backward. His eyes were deep, glowing red, like jewels from the pit of hell itself. He had no lips or nose, and his teeth seemed to consume his entire face. He was tall and muscular, a true monster in every sense of the word. In his enormous, monstrous hands he held three orbs: The first orb appeared to be made entirely of wind, as if he was holding a tiny cyclone in his hand. The second was made out of a brilliant bright light. The third seemed to repel light as if it was the one thing in the universe that light refused to shine upon.

On the goddess's right side stood a creature better looking than the first, but still there was a great deceptive darkness about him. Just by his looks and body movement, one could tell that his soul was probably darker than the monster. Like the goddess and the monster, he had no garments. He had long hair and a strange, deceptive look about him. A dark light surrounded him, and he held two orbs. The first was made out of water. The second was made of ice and was almost as cold as he looked.

Judging from the orbs in their hands, General Vang Kai knew that these three must have been responsible for the destruction upon Washington DC, Ottawa, Brasilia, Buenos Aires, and Moscow.

The goddess creature walked down from of the hill of rubble that used to be a van and walked straight up to General Vang Kai and Huiliang. Huiliang thought that she could breathe easy. After all, how could such a beautiful creature be evil?

General Vang Kai knew better. The goddess walked up to General Vang Kai and said, "You must be the one in charge here. Your garments give you away."

General Vang Kai simply replied yes.

While looking at the stars on his uniform, she continued. "I see you are well versed in worshipping things that shine in the sky. Good. Now, where is the orb of fire?"

General Vang Kai knew what she was looking for, but he also knew that he was sworn to protect it. "I do not know what you are talking about," he replied.

"Really?" the goddess asked. She turned to the cold-looking being and said, "Aris, the old man and the girl I may need. The others are expendable. Would you please kill them?"

Aris replied, "As you wish, Luminous." Suddenly the Chinese soldiers who had accompanied General Vang Kai and Huiliang were decapitated faster than the human eye could catch.

Huiliang's heart was full of fear and dread as she clung close to her uncle.

Luminous turned back to General Vang Kai and said, "My apologies. Maybe I wasn't being quite clear. Let me spell it out for you. You see, I am what you would call an aspiring orb collector, and the problem is that without your orb, I find my collection incomplete. So you see, we have a problem here as long as you refuse to give me what I need. Oh, and by the way, don't try denying that you have it. We know it's here somewhere. The problem is that we don't know exactly where it is. I respect you for that; not too many people could fool our senses. I will ask you one more time. Where is the orb of fire?"

Judging by her statements, General Vang Kai knew that the cloaking device was at least partially successful. Still, he knew that whatever this alien wanted the orb for wasn't good. "I already told you, I do not know what you are talking about."

Luminous was losing patience. "Fine, then. Be that way!" She turned to Huiliang. "Perhaps this girl will be able to persuade you to talk."

For once in his life, General Vang Kai was afraid—not for himself but for Huiliang.

Suddenly the rest of the Chinese Red Guard showed up, surrounding the group with automatic weapons, RPGs, and tanks. "We are the Red Guard! Surrender immediately, or we will open fire!"

Luminous, Aris, and the hideous monster that accompanied them didn't seem to take the Red Guard seriously. The monster turned to Luminous and asked anxiously, "Can I kill them?"

Luminous acted as if this was just another day at the office. "Oh, go ahead, Dagan."

After setting his orbs on the ground, Dagan immediately leapt into action. He ran straight toward the Chinese military like a lion running toward a flock of sheep. All military units immediately opened fire, but Dagan ran straight through the artillery barrage and the hail of bullets as if they were shooting at him with water pistols. The monster ripped through the tanks as if they were made of foil. Several MIG fighter jets opened fire on Dagan, only to realize that the attack did absolutely nothing.

Dagan leapt from the earth, landing on one of the MIGs. He ran his monstrous hand straight through the cockpit glass, grabbing the pilot's head and crushing it in his hand. Then he tore the jet apart in midair, jumping off only before it crashed.

As Aris watched the battle, he turned to Luminous and asked, "Why is he just playing around? We have work to do."

Luminous calmly replied, "Let him have his fun."

Dagan grabbed one of the tanks and threw it toward the Chinese soldiers, crushing them under it like insects. Several more Chinese soldiers opened fire, only to be torn limb from limb.

As General Vang Kai saw the pride of the Red Guard being ripped apart in front of his eyes, he realized China was doomed. The few surviving Chinese soldiers attempted to retreat but were hunted down and killed in rapid succession.

After the massacre, Luminous turned back to General Vang Kai. "Now then, where were we? Oh, yes—you were just about to tell me where to find the orb you misplaced."

General Vang Kai stood his ground. "I told you before, I don't know what you are talking about."

"Really? Okay, then, I guess we came to the wrong place." Luminous turned her attention to Huiliang. "But before I go, something still puzzles me. Tell me, why do you people hang cloth on your bodies? Is it to protect your pale, putrid skin?"

With that Huiliang's nightgown and bathrobe completely disintegrated, and she was left standing naked in front of them.

Her uncle tried to cover her with his military jacket, but the monstrous Dagan grabbed him by the back of the neck and threw him away from her.

Tears came to Huiliang's face as she tried to cover herself with her hands.

Dagan laughed as if he was watching a comedy. Aris had a disgustingly pleasurable look on his face.

General Vang Kai could barely stand the sight of his niece helpless and violated by these monsters.

Luminous could tell that Vang Kai was almost at his limit. She turned back toward Huiliang and said to Aris and Dagan, "I wonder why these humans are so forgetful? Perhaps it has something to do with their ape brains. Perhaps we should dissect one and find out."

Vang Kai could not stand this any longer. "Enough! If I show you where the orb is, do you promise to leave us in peace?"

"If you give me the orb, I promise to leave you, the girl, and this country in peace. You have my word," replied Luminous.

General Vang Kai walked up to Huiliang, put his jacket on her, and tried to comfort her as much as possible. He took Luminous, Aris, Dagan, and Huiliang to a top-secret Chinese military lab. The Chinese soldiers standing guard immediately pointed their weapons at Luminous, Aris, and Dagan. With just a thought, Luminous put all the Chinese soldiers to sleep.

Dagan again asked Luminous, "Can I kill them too?"

"No!" Luminous replied firmly. "I have given my word. As long as they hold up their end of the bargain, you are not to kill anyone. Understood?"

The monstrous Dagan acted like a scolded little boy.

Vang Kai took the group to a heavily armored safe room, where the orb of fire rested on a pedestal. Aris snatched it up immediately.

Luminous smiled a beautiful yet evil smile as she said, "Six down; two to go. This is going easier than I thought."

While holding Huiliang close to him, General Vang Kai said, "You have what you came for. Now, leave us in peace!"

Turning to Aris, Luminous said sarcastically, "Being a human must be more miserable than I thought. They're so forgetful. They hang rags on their bodies, and now they are deliberately asking me to kill them." She turned her back to Vang Kai. "Oh, unless I wasn't being clear earlier? Sorry, my bad. I keep forgetting I need to explain every detail to you apes. See, when I said that I would leave you in peace, I was referring to eternal peace."

All General Vang Kai could think about was protecting Huiliang. He immediately ordered her to get behind him. Then he pulled out his handgun and opened fire on Luminous. The bullets simply bounced off her beautiful white skin as if Vang Kai was trying to kill her with a water pistol.

In the blink of an eye, the monster Dagan ripped Vang

Kai's heart from his chest and crushed it in his cruel, monstrous hand.

With her uncle dead, Huiliang now stood before the monster Dagan.

Dagan smiled, showing his enormous, hideous teeth. He relished what he was about to do. "Just like a little doll. I love breaking dolls."

Huiliang knew she was already dead.

Suddenly a brilliant burst of light shot through the armored wall of the safe room and hit Dagan, sending him flying into the wall opposite. There before Huiliang stood the most attractive man she had ever seen. Like Luminous and the others, this one had no garments. He looked as if he was carved out of solid steel, and he had the type of form one would expect a Greek god or Superman to have. He had beautiful, long blue hair, and his entire body gave off a brilliant blue light. Huiliang couldn't help but stare at the beautiful, heroic figure that now stood between her and Luminous.

For a few brief moments, Luminous and Huiliang's rescuer stood glaring at each other, as if the two of them were old enemies and hated rivals. Almost immediately another warrior effortlessly punched through the armored walls of the safe room and landed beside Huiliang's rescuer. This one looked similar to the first—or at least, they seemed to be part of the same species. His armored body gave off a glorious green glow, and he was taller and more muscular than the first, like a body-builder god. These two stood shoulder to shoulder in a stare-down against Luminous and Aris, with Huiliang behind them.

Almost immediately the glorious green warrior turned to Huiliang's rescuer and said, "Tal, we can't win this! We need to withdraw now!"

Huiliang's rescuer, Tal, immediately grabbed her. While holding her close to his chest, he flew straight through the armored ceiling of the roof. Beijing loomed below them as they shot into the air like bullets.

Huiliang didn't know whether this was reality or some kind of glorious dream. With Tal holding her close, she was flying through the night at impossible speed. The landscape in front of her disappeared behind her in seconds.

The glorious green warrior, Siegfried, flew beside them. Siegfried looked back and could see the monstrous Dagan in hot pursuit. He thought to himself, *Only Dagan? Between me and Tal, we could probably finish him off easily enough.* After looking at Huiliang in Tal's arms, he reconsidered. *No. If we try to take on Dagan, that mortal girl will probably die in the process. I guess we have no choice but to run for now. But still, why would Luminous only sent Dagan after us? What is she up to?*

Back inside the safe room of the Chinese laboratory, Luminous smiled. "Well, it's about time. For a minute I was afraid I'd get all the orbs before they even got here."

Aris, who was using his energy to make the orbs float around him like balloons, seemed worried. "Why did you let Dagan go off like that? Together the sons of thunder could probably defeat him."

"Not as long as they're carrying that human trash with them. Well, it's a dirty job, but I suppose someone has to do it. Besides, Dagan is an idiot and is expendable. If he wants to get himself killed, who are we to stand in his way?"

Aris still seemed worried. "Are you sure this plan of yours will work?"

Luminous looked at Aris with a slightly hateful face. "Are you questioning me?"

Aris knew he'd stepped over the line and said apologetically, "No, Your Highness."

A smile returned to Luminous's face. "Good. Then let's get back to the Spirex. After all, we have to make Veritalon's funeral arrangements." Just before she and Aris left, she said very casually, "Oh, I almost forgot. I have a promise to keep." With just a thought from Luminous, Beijing was leveled like Washington DC and the other capitals. "I hate being reduced to pest control. Oh well. At least we made the universe a cleaner place today. Now, come on. We have things to do."

Luminous and Aris flew back toward Washington with the orbs in tow.

Dagan was still chasing Siegfried, Tal, and Huiliang. Siegfried saw the Himalayas in the distance, and he turned to Tal. "We'll lose him in that rocky outcropping!"

"Right!" Tal exclaimed.

The two of them dove sharply toward the mountains.

Dagan, blinded by his rage, immediately followed after them.

Siegfried turned to Tal. "Split up! Get that girl to safety! I've got this!"

"Gotcha! You take care, brother!"

Siegfried and Tal headed in opposite directions.

At first Dagan was chasing Tal and Huiliang—until Siegfried shot him in the back. When Dagan turned around, Siegfried mocked him. "You always were stupid. Now you're stupid and ugly!"

Infuriated, Dagan started chasing Siegfried.

As the two of them began to approach Mount Everest, Siegfried shot the top of the enormous mountain off, sending it crashing down between them. Dagan hit the enormous mountaintop aside as if he was swatting a fly. But when the huge boulder no longer obstructed his view, Siegfried was nowhere to be seen. "Damn you! Where are you? Show yourself, coward!"

Down at the base of the mountain, Siegfried was slowly and quietly moving the top of the boulder off of his body. He had latched on to it when Dagan hit it aside. Far above him, he could hear Dagan cursing. As Siegfried slowly walked away into the darkness, he gave a half smile as he said, "See you around, Dagan."

Halfway around the world in New York City, Victor Landgard, owner of the multinational Landgard Corporation and the man most favored to win the presidency that year, was giving his election speech. It was the usual spiel about how if people elected him into office, there would be improvements and lower taxes.

Suddenly the secret service agents that were protecting him came up to the stage and asked everyone to leave immediately. "Please come with us, Mr. President."

Victor Landgard was puzzled. "I'm not president yet."

"You are now."

As Victor Landgard was escorted to his limousine by the secret service, he could see multitudes of people in a state of panic. Inside he asked the agent sitting across from him, "What the hell is going on?"

The agent grimly reported, "Washington DC has been hit."

Victor Landgard breathed a heavy breath, as if he had the weight of the world on his shoulders. For the United States to declare him president before elections, he knew it had to be bad. "Was it nuclear? Are we at war?"

"We don't know the details. You will be taken to a safe location, where you will be briefed on the situation."

Mr. Landgard reclined back into the leather seat of the limousine. As he put his head back and stared at the ceiling, he knew that this would be the longest day of his life.

– CHAPTER TWO –

Humanity's Best-kept Secret

AS THE NEWS OF WASHINGTON DC, BEIJING, and the other capitals leaked out through social media and the press, people all over the world began to panic. In the major cities highways were jammed. Riots and looters took anything they could get their hands on, and police were hard-pressed to keep order.

In a city not too far from the rubble of Washington, a man, his wife, and his eight-year-old daughter entered the back room of their store. The store had been in their family for years; now looters were breaking in and taking everything they had worked so hard to achieve. The man took his daughter and hid her in a tiny cabinet behind some wooden pallets. "It's going to be all right, Anna!" he said, stroking her yellow hair. "You just stay here and keep quiet!" He shut the door.

Inside, Anna could hear the screams of her mother and father. Too afraid and heartbroken to even cry, Anna went numb as she put her hands over her ears, trying desperately to wake up from this nightmare.

Back at Mount Everest, Dagan was still cursing Siegfried. He heard a familiar voice behind him. "Damn, you're loud," said the voice sarcastically.

Immediately Dagan's eyes were full of shock and fear. As he turned around, there in front of him stood another warrior similar looking to Tal and Siegfried, but there was something dark and deformed about this one.

Like Tal and Siegfried, he radiated light, but his light seemed darker in nature. Like Tal, he had long hair and wore a cold-looking iron mask over his mouth. His entire right arm looked like it belonged on a demon and not on a beautiful warrior. The skin on the arm looked like old brown leather, and blood vessels pumped glowing, deep-red blood through the arm all the way up to his neck, where it disappeared behind his iron mask. He looked as if he was a cross between good and evil.

When Dagan saw him, he looked as if he had seen a dead man. "Rilic! You can't be here—you're dead!" exclaimed Dagan, full of fear.

"Now, is that any way to talk to an old friend?" Rilic replied sarcastically.

"Rilic, I swear I had nothing to do with it!"

"Oh, come on. You had *everything* to do with it. Well, not everything, but you know what I mean. But let's not dwell on the past. Instead, let's focus on the future. Which brings me to my first question. How many orbs does Luminous have?"

"I don't know!"

No sooner did Dagan finish the sentence than he found himself crying out in pain. Using his right demon arm, Rilic broke Dagan's arm. "Sorry, not the answer I'm looking for. I'll ask you one more time. How many orbs does Luminous have?"

Dagan was silent. Suddenly he screamed in pain as Rilic broke his other arm. "Six! She has six!" Dagan finally admitted.

"Which six does she have?"

"All but the orbs of life and death."

"That was surprisingly easy. So what is she really up to?"

Once again Dagan was silent. Rilic punched Dagan in the gut. As the monstrous Dagan crumpled to the ground, Rilic stood over him.

"You know, I'm really getting tired of the silent treatment. I keep asking the questions, but you don't pay any attention. What's Luminous really up to?"

Dagan looked Rilic straight in the eye and said, "No, you have no idea what's coming—and I will die before I tell the likes of you!"

Rilic was surprised for a moment but then regained his composure. "Die? Well, if that's your preference." With that, Rilic used his right demon arm and ripped Dagan's heart from his chest.

Dagan's heart and body turned to burned ashes and blew away on the wind.

Rilic looked down at His right demon arm and said, "Not bad."

Somewhere in the United States, Victor Landgard entered a top-secret presidential bunker. As he entered, everyone saluted except for three people who stood apart from the rest: a seasoned-looking, four-star general; an older man, presumably a scientist, based on his attire; and a very attractive Hispanic woman, holding some folders close to her chest.

The general walked up to Victor Landgard and extended his hand as he introduced himself. "General Nathan Staten, United States Marines."

Victor Landgard took his hand and gave it a firm shake. "Victor Landgard. It's an honor, General."

With that General Staten introduced the older gentleman. "This is Doctor Alain Eugene Smith. He probably knows more about what we are dealing with than anyone on the planet."

"Most people just call me Dr. Smith," said the doctor while extending his hand.

"I'll try to remember that. Good to meet you, Doctor," Victor said as he shook Dr. Smith's hand.

Dr. Smith introduced Victor Landgard to the attractive woman standing beside him. "This is Lucia, my associate."

"It's a pleasure to meet you, Miss Lucia."

Lucia was the only one who didn't shake Victor's hand, mainly due to the stack of papers she was holding. "Same here. I only wish it was under more pleasant circumstances."

As the four of them walked down the corridor, heading for the underground war room, they assessed the situation. Victor Landgard turned to Dr. Smith. "Okay, you know more about what's going on here than anyone, so what exactly is going on?"

For a brief moment Dr. Smith looked at General Staten, who looked back with a face that seemed to say, "Fill him in." The doctor replied, "Mr. Landgard, what I am about to tell you may sound like the stuff of science fiction, but I guarantee you all of it is true. Less than an hour ago, Washington DC was wiped from the face of the earth in a matter of seconds."

Victor Landgard nodded. "Yes, they already told me."

"But what they didn't tell you was that Washington wasn't the only one. Ottawa, Brasilia, Buenos Aires, Beijing, and even Moscow are gone."

Victor Landgard was stunned. "How could anyone do that?"

"Well, it wasn't anyone from this world."

"What?"

"Our world has been invaded. From what we can tell,

they seem to be beings evolved from pure energy. Somehow they were able to channel this energy through their bodies. That's how they were able to destroy Washington. In much the same way as a star has multiple layers of energy to keep it running, these beings' bodies contain the same type of systems."

Victor Landgard interrupted. "Wait a minute. Are you saying we're being invaded by aliens from outer space with superpowers?"

"That is correct," Dr. Smith said.

"Forgive me if I misunderstood. Is this some kind of joke?"

General Staten interrupted. "I can assure you this is very real."

Dr. Smith continued. "Don't look so surprised, Mr. Landgard. We are the only sentient species on this planet among all the other animals. One might say we have the superpower of intelligence. Our life forms are carbon-based, so why couldn't there be life forms that are energy-based? Don't close your mind to the possibilities."

Victor Landgard put his hands in his pockets and gave a heavy sigh. "Okay. It's a little hard to swallow, but okay. So these aliens are bombing all of our capitals. Why? Why come here? What do we have that they could possibly want?"

General Staten interjected. "It's better to show you."

The four of them continued to walk down the corridor until they reached the war room. Once inside, they sat down around the presidential conference table.

Lucia dimmed the lights as General Staten turned on

the large flat-screen TV. Staten turned to Victor. "What I'm about to tell you is the oldest and most carefully guarded secret in the history of mankind."

Victor listened intently as General Staten showed him the slideshow on the large screen.

"Around the year 10,000 BC, the early Egyptians found something. Nobody knows exactly what it is, but the Egyptians believed that it was a piece of Ra."

"The Egyptian sun god?" Victor asked.

"Correct," said Lucia. "What they found was a orb completely composed of photons, but more than that, you could actually hold it in your hands."

"Like a lightbulb," added Victor.

Dr. Smith interjected. "No, this orb was made *entirely* of photons. Technically, holding pure light in the palm of your hand is scientifically impossible. Yet with what the Egyptians found, they could do it. We call this object the photon generator, but we don't really know what it is."

General Staten continued. "Through the years, countries have been at war over this object. The Babylonians took it from the Egyptians, the Persians took it from Babylonians, the Greeks took it from the Persians, the Romans took it from the Greeks, the British took it when Rome fell, and then we smuggled it out of Britain when the United States declared its independence. Ever since then, it has remained in Washington as a top-secret national treasure. In the years that followed, we discovered that there was more than one."

Victor said, "More than one? How many?"

"No one really knows. Ever since the turn of

the twenty-first century, the United States has been attempting to collaborate with nations that we assumed had an orb in their possession. The United Nations was actually established in order to achieve that goal, but no country admitted to having one. Now it's safe to say that the countries that were attacked probably had an orb."

"So these aliens dropped these orbs on our planet more than ten thousand years ago, and now they want them back."

"That would appear to be the case," the general conceded.

"Well, the orbs aside, these aliens are clearly hostile. So how do we fight them? What weapons do we have?"

Dr. Smith put in his two cents. "Ever since the industrial revolution, we have found ways of channeling the energy that the photon generator produces. Lucia and I have been working on a crude but effective device that stores the energy given off by the photon generator; we named it the photon battery. It was meant to be used as a free source of energy for the planet. However, it could be deployed as a weapon."

"And where is this photon battery?" asked Victor.

"Well, that's the bad news. It's in Washington."

"So you're saying it was destroyed?"

"No," said Lucia. "The energy signature is still active. If we can recover it, we might have what we need to fight them."

Victor Landgard got up from his seat. "Okay, General. I want the best team we have to go in and get that device ASAP."

General Staten replied, "I'm afraid it isn't that simple. We've detected some sort of crystal spire in Washington. We believe it's the aliens' base of operations."

"Okay, so will need a diversion. Get the team together and call up the F-18s. These aliens showed us some of their weapons. I think it's time we show them some of ours."

In India, in a remote wildlife sanctuary, a glorious warrior stroked the fur of an Indian tiger. This being was the same as Tal and Siegfried, except for the fact that this one was female. Her hair was a beautiful shade of golden yellow, and golden light emanated from her body.

As Tal, Siegfried, and Huiliang landed beside her, the tiger disappeared into the jungle. The woman turned to Tal and Siegfried and said, "You boys scared the tiger away. I take it the two of you weren't able to recover the orb?"

"No. Luminous beat us to it," reported Siegfried.

"How many has she been able to get?"

"It looks like she has all but two."

"Well, this day just keeps getting better and better."

Huiliang, full of shock and disbelief, finally spoke up. "Please, who are you people? What is happening?"

"Who is this?" asked the golden-haired female warrior.

"A local," answered Tal. "We saved her. The others weren't so lucky."

"Please, what is going on?" Huiliang repeated.

The golden-haired warrior turned to Tal. "Tell her. She needs to know."

Huiliang listened intently as Tal told her everything.

"My name is Tal. This is my brother, Siegfried. The one with the golden hair is Aerial. We come from a world far above your own. We call it the eternal realm; I believe you refer to it as heaven. Your world is in the middle of a war between Veritalon, whom we serve, and Luminous.

"It all began long ago, before your sun burned in your sky. Back then, as now, a great infinite power created and ruled the universe. Some call it fate; others call it destiny. I believe your people call it God. He—or rather, it—created Luminous. She was different back then. The great power created her as a being of justice and power. After creating Luminous, the great power created the rest of us as guardians to watch over and protect all of creation, which the Almighty made with eight orbs: fire, wind, water, ice, light, darkness, death, and life.

"Four eons we guardians, led by Luminous, kept the peace. At that time Luminous was the most beautiful and powerful among us. Whole armies turned and ran away at the mention of her name. But with each new victory, she became more and more like the very evil she fought against. One day she decided that she should be the one in charge, not the creator. She convinced one-third of us to join her in revolt, including four of our finest. Her plan was to steal the eight orbs and then destroy and rebuild the universe in her image. In order to defeat her, the creator reincarnated a piece of himself into a body like ours; he became Veritalon. With him on our side, we managed to defeat Luminous and her followers. Luminous and the rest were locked away in a parallel universe of darkness—I believe you would call it hell. The orbs were sent here long before any life existed on this planet. A guardian was sent to keep this world a secret so no one would know where the orbs were hidden.

"But now Luminous has somehow escaped along with the two warriors that you saw. She somehow found the guardian of earth and tricked him into telling her where the orbs were before she killed him. We have been sent to keep the orbs from her until Veritalon arrives."

By the time Tal was done telling the story, Huiliang's eyes were wide and her jaw nearly dropped.

"I'm sorry. This all must be very strange for you," Tal noted.

"Just a little!" answered Huiliang, still stunned by what Tal had told her.

As Tal was explained everything to Huiliang, Aerial and Siegfried listened from a distance. Aerial's thoughts went back in time to a month earlier. Out of all the other guardians, she was the closest one to the guardian of earth, Rilic. Rilic and Aerial had a relationship far deeper than mere friendship. Lately Rilic had become very distant. Every time Aerial tried to approach him for any reason, Rilic shut down. Then word had arrived that Luminous had escaped and Rilic was dead. It didn't take a genius to work out what had happened. Back before Luminous rebelled, Rilic had taken a liking to her, both as a warrior and a woman. Aerial knew that her lover, Rilic, had betrayed earth to Luminous before she'd killed him. Aerial hurt even more deeply because before the rebellion, she herself looked up to Luminous as a role model and hero. Now both her lover and her hero had betrayed everything in which they believed.

Back at Mount Everest, Rilic was still looking at his right demon arm, and he also thought back on the events that had led him to this point in time. Back then, he didn't have a right demon arm or a mask over his mouth; he was like Tal, Siegfried, and Aerial.

When Luminous first started her rebellion against the creator, Rilic had every intention of joining her, but fear of the creator's power kept him from joining. After Luminous and her conspirators were imprisoned by Veritalon, Rilic himself was put in charge of the eight orbs of creation and was entrusted with their location: earth. In the centuries that passed, Rilic began to forget all about Luminous, and he developed a deep, intimate relationship with another female warrior whom he respected, Aerial. But when Luminous escaped, all those ancient desires quickly returned.

For the last several days, Luminous continued to visit Rilic on a secluded asteroid, far from any listening ears. Many times she tried to get Rilic to reveal the location of the orbs. Then one horrible night, she succeeded.

When Rilic and Luminous were alone, she approached him. "I don't understand. You trust me enough to not tell anyone we are together, and yet you don't trust me enough to tell me where the orbs are."

"Because I know what you plan to do with them. You're going to kill everything."

She gently put both of her soft hands on Rilic's face and said calmly and passionately, "Rilic, you and I both know that the universe is imperfect and will always be imperfect as long as imperfect beings live in it. This universe was created by Veritalon, but does he care about it? He simply spins this universe into existence and then walks off and leaves, like a father leaving a discarded child in the gutter. As a result, all the numerous life forms in space fight among themselves. There is war, devastation, and death because of Veritalon's blunder. He is a cold, cruel god. Despite what you and the other guardians think of me, I am not the monster here. Please tell me where they are."

Finally, Rilic gave in. "Earth. They're on earth."

Luminous smiled a beautiful, seductive smile as she said, "Kiss me!"

As Rilic was about to kiss her, her teeth turned into dragonlike fangs. Rilic cried out as Luminous drove her fangs into the side of his neck. Rilic crumpled to the ground as Luminous stood over him. While looking up at his former lover's cold face, he asked, "Why?"

"It's simple, actually. You see, *you* are part of the problem. You and the other guardians." Just then, Aris and Dagan landed beside her. "We know where they are," Luminous told them.

As Luminous's venom began to spread through Rilic's body, he could hear Luminous's mocking voice. "Watching your body liquefy may not be pretty, so if it's all the same with you, I have better things to do."

Luminous, Aris, and Dagan flew off, leaving Rilic to die.

As the poison continued to spread; Rilic could feel it creeping up to his mouth and his right arm. He knew it was only a matter of time before his body changed and then decayed, until nothing of him remained.

Then suddenly and unexpectedly, Rilic saw a vision of Veritalon walking toward him. As Veritalon approached; Rilic began to tremble out of fear and shame. Veritalon spoke with a voice that resonated power and authority, but most of all disappointment. "Rilic, what have you done?"

"It's not my fault. She tricked me!" replied Rilic in his own defense.

"Did she? You knew all along that she was the enemy. Now you have thrown away every gift I ever gave you. The heart of a woman who loves you. The great future I had planned for you. And now because of your actions, an innocent world is about to die. All this because you lusted after darkness!"

"I am about to pay for my crime with my life. Isn't that punishment enough?"

"No, it is not! Your single life does not equal the billions that will die because of your actions!" Veritalon stretched out his hand, and the venom that was consuming Rilic's body stopped, leaving Rilic with his deformed right demon arm and a deformed mouth. "Now you must live with your crimes. And know this: for what you have done, you shall never have Aerial's heart again. She shall give it to one more worthy than you. You shall never know what it's like to be loved by a woman again, save for one. One who is not a woman but a child without a family. Only she can redeem you. Love her as a father should, and then and only then will you be fully restored." Then Veritalon disappeared as mysteriously as he came.

Rilic's thoughts turned to the present. He stared at his right demon arm, pondering what Veritalon had told him. Then his thoughts turned to Luminous and what she'd done to him. Rilic spoke to himself very cold and calmly. "Okay, that's enough reminiscing for one day. I've got things to do and a bitch to kill."

On a United States Marines base a few miles from Washington, the team that was assigned to recover the photon battery was preparing to move out. The team was led by General Nathan Staten's own son, Captain James Staten. Among the team were two of James's war buddies.

Sergeant Nathan Johnson was tough as nails and a no-nonsense guy in every sense of the word. He was the type of man one didn't want to piss off.

The second was Corporal Danny Roberson, but everyone called him Stumpy: he was the opposite, the type of guy who would twist a knot in the devil's tail just for a joke.

Together these three had seen many hard times together, including fighting in the heart of Afghanistan. Ultimately the men survived many times when their friends did not.

The rest of the unit stood at attention in single file as

Captain James Staten addressed them. "All right, ladies, the mission is simple and straightforward. We go in, retrieve the package, get out, and kill anyone or anything that gets in our way. No matter what you run into, remember this: for more than two hundred years, our corps has done two things for this nation—we make marines, and we win wars! Never forget that! You're marines, and not all the demons in hell can overrun you! Hurrah!"

Every man shouted, "Hurrah!"

"Move out, devil dogs!"

With that the unit headed for Washington.

– CHAPTER THREE –

Aris's Blunder

I N THE CRYSTAL SPIRE, OR THE SPIREX, LUMINOUS sat on a beautiful, ornate crystal throne in the center of a very large crystal room. She smiled as she looked at the sight before her. There in front of her were four warriors in a state of deep meditation as they channeled their energy into a crystal that hovered in the center of them.

The first warrior was named Facade. She appeared to be no more than a little girl, except for the fact that she looked dead. Her skin was too pale to belong to anyone alive. Her hair was black with shades of deep green. But above all, her eyes were the most frightening features. Looking into them was like looking into a empty pit.

The second warrior was named Inferno. She was

very attractive, but something about her seemed hungry, all-consuming.

The third was Rampage. He was tall and muscular. He had an elongated head, and spikes came out of his shoulders and chest. The spikes seemed to glow, as if his bones had an unearthly energy within them. His skin looked more like cement then anything. All in all, this giant looked less like a warrior and more like a fortress with legs, a towering machine with deadly weapons.

The fourth and final member of the group was named Vartile. He was far taller than anyone in the group but also far thinner. One could see his muscles as if he had no skin anywhere. His fingernails resembled long and very sharp claws, which seemed to take up all the room his hands had to offer.

These four were the finest warriors that Tal had mentioned to Huiliang, but now they were simply known as the four warriors of the Apocalypse.

Luminous smiled while watching her plan come together. Across the room, Aris, who was watching the orbs, had deep concerns about her plan. "Are you sure this is wise, my queen? Shouldn't we be looking for the rest of the orbs?"

"They'll be plenty of time for that later. I didn't just come all this way just to make the universe a better place. I have to wait for Veritalon to get here—my vengeance would not be complete without him! After he's dead and we have no more competition, we can take our time finding the last two orbs."

Aris was still concerned. "Forgive me, my queen, but

if this plan is foolproof, why do you have those two among the humans?"

"Never underestimate your opponent, especially when it's Veritalon. If this plan does fail, we'll need insurance."

Luminous stepped off her throne and put all of Ari's fears to rest. While touching his face and looking deep into his eyes, she said, "Don't worry. Everything will go my way." Then she reassumed her position back on the throne.

Tal left Huiliang alone with her thoughts as he assessed the situation with Siegfried and Aerial. "So Luminous only sent Dagan after you boys?" asked Aerial.

"That's right," replied Siegfried.

"What could she be up to?"

"I don't know. But whatever it is, I don't like it."

"What about the four?" Aerial asked.

Siegfried said, "There was no sign of them. I'm guessing they didn't escape."

"Well, at least that's one piece of good news."

Tal piped in. "Excuse me, but aren't we missing the point? Luminous has six of the eight orbs. If she gets her hands on the last two before Veritalon gets here, the next battle will be over before it begins."

"All right, we'll have to find the last two before Luminous does," answered Siegfried. "She's probably heading for the closest one, which is not too far from here. We'll head for the farthest one."

Looking in the direction of Australia, Aerial replied, "Its last known position was in that direction."

Tal looked toward Huiliang and asked, "What about her? We can't just leave her here."

"One of us will have to stay behind and look after her," said Aerial.

Siegfried said, "Tal, she seems to have formed a bond with you. You'll stay behind while Aerial and I retrieve the orb."

Tal nodded his head. He grabbed Siegfried's forearm and said, "You two take care of yourselves!"

"Don't worry, brother. We've been through some scrapes in the past, and we're going to get through this one."

With that, Siegfried and Aerial took to the skies, leaving Tal and Huiliang alone together.

At the Taj Mahal, Rilic landed outside of the enormous structure. The security guards shied away but kept a close eye on him as he entered.

In the presidential bunker, General Nathan Staten walked up to President Landgard. "Sir, we have satellite confirmation that one of the aliens is in India at the Taj Mahal as we speak."

"Put it on the screen," said Victor.

Rilic was now inside the Taj Mahal and standing before a tomb. He reached out his right demon arm. A strangely beautiful orb of death passed through the walls of the tomb and came directly into Rilic's hand. Well, here's one orb that conniving little bitch won't get her grubby little hands on."

As Rilic was leaving, the security guards opened fire. The bullets had no effect on Rilic. *Still playing with toys? When are these stupid little people going to grow up?* He exited the structure.

Victor Landgard, General Staten, Doctor Smith, and Lucia could see him on the screen. "So that's what we're up against," said Victor.

Inside the Spirex, Luminous was suddenly shocked and confused.

"What's wrong, my queen?" asked Aris.

"Rilic—he's still alive!"

"But how is that possible? You killed him yourself. I saw it!"

"I don't know. But him being here was not part of the plan. I have to finish him—now!"

"Please, my queen, allow me."

"No. You're good, but Rilic's better. Stay here and protect the orbs. I will finish Rilic myself."

"As you wish, my queen."

Luminous shot out of the Spirex, heading for India as fast as her wings could carry her. But by the time she got there, Rilic was already gone.

The satellite that was locked on to Rilic lost him as well. "Where did that alien disappear to?" demanded President Landgard.

A soldier reported, "We don't know, sir. He was there one minute, and the next he was gone."

"Okay, keep the satellite trained on that female. But I want that first one found."

"Understood, sir."

Luminous scoured the area looking for Rilic. Unknown to her, Rilic was watching her from the bottom of the Yamuna River. "All right, how did that bitch know where I was?" Rilic thought to himself until he had an idea. "Wait a minute. If Luminous is here, then the only one guarding the orbs is Aris. Well, looks like this has all the makings of my lucky day." Rilic snuck away, leaving Luminous to play a global scale of hide-and-seek.

Huiliang wore a beautiful garment that shined like the stars. Tal had materialized it for her because she had nothing else but her uncle's uniform. Now she held the uniform nicely folded in her hands. Upon recalling his death, tears fell from her eyes.

Tal returned from saying good-bye to Siegfried and Aerial. Huiliang immediately attempted to dry her eyes as Tal said, "I'm sorry."

Huiliang began to think out loud. "After my father and mother were killed, my uncle promised my father that he would look after me. Now everyone I love is gone."

As Huiliang wept, Tal held her head close to his chest. For several minutes, the two of them said nothing but held each other close.

Finally Tal spoke. "I know it's hard now. But when Veritalon arrives, everything will be set right."

"Can he bring back the dead?" a grief-filled Huiliang asked.

"Yes, he can."

Huiliang looked up at Tal. Her eyes seemed to say, "How?"

Tal explained. "He has a code by which he lives. He does not interfere in the natural development of worlds, whether that development is good or evil. He lets the inhabitants of planets make their own decisions. That being said, he will not bring back anyone that is killed by their own species or a species that is indigenous to the planet. But if an alien race invades another world or interferes in any level, then he may step in. I have seen him restore entire worlds that have been burnt, and that includes bringing back the dead. Your uncle was killed by Dagan. So yes, you will see him again. That's a promise."

Huiliang could hardly believe what she heard. It was a fragile hope, but it was hope nonetheless. Taking into account everything she had seen, she was not about to dismiss a miracle.

Siegfried and Aerial arrived in the outback of Australia. Upon landing, they were surprised at what they saw. A multitude of people were camping out and taking refuge in this vast land. The people seemed to be expecting them, looking at Siegfried and Aerial as if they were saviors.

Finally the crowd parted as the shaman approached Siegfried and Aerial. "You two are from the dream time."

Siegfried and Aerial looked at each other out of surprise, and then they turned back to the shaman. "How could you possibly know that?" asked Siegfried.

"That is of little importance now. We have so very little time, my friends." The shaman handed the ancient ornate box to Siegfried. "This is what she wants. I feel it will be safer in your hands than in mine."

Siegfried opened the box. Within it was the orb of life.

"Thank you," said Aerial.

"Do not thank me. This journey is far from over. You believe that when the great one arrives, this conflict will pass, but I sense once he arrives, the darkness will only grow deeper. The snake will shed her skin, and the dragon will rise. But for all of you, this battle will take a heavy toll. All of your dreams and hopes of the one who will save you will die in front of you. But fear not—it is darkest just before dawn. I have said far too much and have taken up far too much time. You two must go now! If you want to save our world, you must hurry! Rejoin your friends!"

Siegfried and Aerial nodded as they took to the air, bringing the orb of life with them. Aerial turned to Siegfried. "Okay, that was weird."

"Tell me about it. I had no idea these people could master the sight," Siegfried replied.

"And what he said°... What do you think it means?"Aerial asked, full of concern.

"I have no idea. I'll think about that once we get this orb to safety."

Inside the Spirex, Aris paced back and forth, the words of Luminous still ringing in his ears. "No. You're good, but Rilic's better." Aris thought to himself, *If it wasn't for the orbs, would she still be with me? What does she think of me? Who does she think I am? I can handle Rilic! She wants to see him again. Why?*

Unexpectedly, he heard a voice speaking to him. "Can Aris come out to play?" It was Rilic himself, taunting Aris telepathically.

"Rilic!"

"Nice to talk to you to, Aris. Although I'd rather talk to you face-to-face. That is, unless you prefer hiding out in that big crystal thing. Oh, by the way, you don't have to worry about your little playmate Dagan. I sent him on a vacation to the afterlife—one-way, of course. One more thing, before I forget. I've also found something that belongs to Veritalon. I took the liberty of putting it in a safe location. After all, wouldn't want anyone wandering off with it."

"You have an orb?"

"Well, now, you've heard everything I just said. Do I have to spell it out for you?"

"Where are you?"

"Glad you asked. I'm right outside."

Aris looked at the four warriors and the orbs for a bit. Then he left the Spirex to meet Aris. Outside, the two of them faced each other.

"Wow. Why does Luminous only recruit the stupid ones? Is that her recruitment policy?" said a cocky Rilic.

"Maybe she leaves the stupid ones to rot! Last time I saw you, you were squirming on the ground like a maggot! Why are you still alive?"

"Oh, I don't know. I just figured death is so boring."

Aris sneered. "Well, as much as I enjoy chatting with you, I've got more important things to do! Where is the orb?"

"Somewhere around."

"I'll kill you if you don't tell me where it is!"

Rilic laughed. "Really? Now, that's a trick I'd like to see."

"Fine, then. Be that way!"

Aris gave Rilic a blow that sent him flying. Rilic could barely pick himself up.

Aris laughed. "I'm really disappointed in you. After all that talk, I thought you'd be a little more challenging than this."

Even though he could barely get on his feet, Rilic laughed as well "You have a woman's touch."

Aris delivered a right hook to Rilic's face, breaking his mask. "I've just about had enough of you! Tell me where you hid the orb!"

Rilic spit up a tooth as he very calmly said, "Go to hell."

Aris delivered another painful blow to Rilic, the force crippling him. "Fine, then!" said Aris; grabbing Rilic by the leg and dragging him into the Spirex. "We'll see how cocky you are before Luminous."

In the presidential bunker, General Staten reported to President Landgard. "Sir, we found the male alien."

"Put it up."

Everyone in the room could see Aris dragging Rilic into the crystal structure.

"What do you think happened there?" asked Lucia.

Doctor Smith shook his head. "Your guess is as good as mine."

President Landgard turned to General Staten. "How long before the F-18s arrive?"

"Shortly."

"Good. Not a moment too soon."

Luminous was still looking for Rilic when she unexpectedly turned and looked in the direction of the Spirex. "No, no! He did not just do that!" She immediately raced back to the Spirex.

Inside the Spirex, Aris dropped Rilic on the ground. Then he heard the sounds of the F-18s bombing the Spirex. As Aris began to walk outside to deal with them, he turned back to Rilic. "Don't run away, now."

Immediately after Aris left, Rilic got back up. "No promises," he said. He looked around the room and almost had a heart attack when he caught a glimpse of the four warriors and what they were doing. "So that's what she's up to," he said, his eyes open wide. He knew he had to get the orbs out of there before the four warriors awoke or Luminous returned. After materializing another mask for himself and putting it on, he grabbed the orbs and rushed outside. Once out, he could hear Aris destroying every F-18 in the sky. As he slowly made his getaway with the orbs, he turned back in the direction of Aris. "I guess you won't be needing these anymore. Have fun."

As Aris cleared the skies, on the other side of the Spirex, Captain James Staten and his unit was clearing the rubble that had fallen on the photon battery. Every man struggled, moving the massive pieces of debris as quickly as possible.

"Move it, marines!" shouted James as he moved faster and harder than anyone. They uncovered it, but unfortunately, it was clear it had been damaged. Captain James hastily picked it up. "Let's get the hell out of here!" The entire unit pulled out, heading for a rendezvous point where two choppers were waiting. Suddenly out of nowhere, one of the F-18s crashed on the spot where Sergeant Nathan Johnson was standing; killing him instantly. Stumpy almost ran back, but James grabbed him by the arm.

"We have to help him!" Stumpy insisted.

James said, "Forget him—he's gone! Now move it, marine! That's an order!"

Finally the unit made it to the choppers. James handed the photon battery to Stumpy and sent him and half of the unit on the first chopper. Then he and the other half got on the second chopper.

Aris noticed the two helicopters leaving. He stretched out his hand and shot down the helicopter that James had boarded. The first one was too far away, and Aris had his hands full.

James's helicopter spun out of control. In all the confusion, Aris had only managed to hit the tail. The helicopter hit the ground in a heap of rubble, killing all inside with the exception of James, who passed out from the impact.

General Nathan Staten was pleased to hear that the unit had recovered the battery, but it was a pleasure short-lived when he heard that his son was missing in action. He reported to President Landgard. "Sir, they have the battery."

"Excellent. Order the F-18s to pull out."

"Yes, sir."

But as General Nathan Staten walked away, President Landgard sensed a deep look of concern on his face. "Is something wrong, General?"

"No, sir," General Staten said as he walked away. "You'd better be all right, boy," Staten said quietly to himself.

In the city not too far from Washington, Anna, the heartbroken little girl, walked down empty streets. Hunger had driven her out from her hiding place, but there was no food to be found; the looters had taken everything. The city looked more like a ghost town, the type one would expect the end of the world to look like. Anna continued to stagger forward through the town, but starvation, depression, and exhaustion took their toll on her. Her beautiful golden hair was now snarled with dust and dirt. Her once cheerful face was dirty and too full of shock to give any expression. Overhead she could hear the sounds of fighter jets; it was the F-18s in full retreat. Anna continued to walk forward like a zombie. Her tiny and weak body was only a shell of the cheerful little girl that had once occupied it.

Captain James Staten finally regained consciousness. All around him were the dead bodies of his unit. He knew he had to get out. After checking every man, he realized he was the only one left. Upon leaving the wreckage of the helicopter behind, he set out alone on foot for the nearest populated city.

Luminous returned to the Spirex only to discover Rilic had stolen all the orbs out from under Aris's nose. Aris bowed before Luminous. His only thought was getting back at Rilic, even as Luminous chewed him out.

"I can't believe this! You were told to stay here and protect the orbs! Now they're gone! They'll be no reason for Veritalon to come to us now, and if he gets his hands on all eight orbs, he'll use their power to seal us up again! All this because you're so stupid! Have I left anything out?"

"Please, my queen. Send me after Rilic. I promise I'll retrieve the orbs and bring you Rilic's head."

Luminous finally calmed down and drew in a deep breath. She walked up to Aris and put her hands on his face as he got up. "Very well. But I expect you to return with both the orbs and Rilic."

"I promise I will not fail you, my queen."

Luminous smiled as she looked deeply and passionately into Aris eyes. "Kiss me."

As Aris moved in close to kiss his beloved queen, suddenly Luminous drove her dragon fangs into his neck. Aris backed up out of fear for his life. "No, no! What are you doing!?" asked Aris as the poison began to eat away at his body.

"It was very stupid of you to disobey my orders," said Luminous coldly. As she walked away and assumed her place back on the throne, Aris dissolved into smoke.

Luminous sat on the throne and contemplated how to turn this around. She realized that the only way to win was to wait for the four warriors to complete the task at hand.

At the wildlife sanctuary, Tal, who was sitting on a log next to Huiliang, rose to his feet. Huiliang did the same as Siegfried, and Aerial returned from their trip with the orb of life.

Tal smiled. "Looks like you guys did okay."

"More than okay," exclaimed Aerial. "You're not going to believe this, but some of these people have the sight."

"Is that even possible?"

Siegfried chimed in. "It is. We've seen it for ourselves."

Aerial continued. "This orb was in the protection of a earth wise man. With him were several other humans out in the wilderness, away from the major cities. He knew somehow that Luminous was coming even before she got here, and he also knew who we were."

Aerial was interrupted when everyone noticed the arrival of Rilic.

"Yes, I'm here, and I'm alive—long story. Listen, we've got big problems."

"How did you find us?" Siegfried asked.

"Oh, I have been aware of your movements since you came to earth. After all, I am the guardian."

Huiliang had no idea what to make of all this, these soldiers of light conversing with a dark being. She never expected the guardian of earth to look like this.

With a side glance at Huiliang, Rilic casually spoke. "So you guys prefer the company of humans now. Oh well, could be worse, I suppose. Anyway, where was I? Oh, yeah: we've got big problems."

"Go on," said Siegfried.

"The four warriors are here. They've been channeling their combined energy into one crystal in an effort to kill Veritalon when he arrives."

"Impossible," said Aerial, not believing a word that came out of Rilic's mouth. "Veritalon's power comes directly from the source of all life. Not even the four warriors and Luminous have that much power."

"No you're not getting it. They've been at this for a very long time. My guess is that they've been at this ever since they were sealed up."

Siegfried said, "But to gather that much power, if Luminous were to detonate it, everything would be destroyed—including Luminous."

"Not if Veritalon uses his own energy to shield the universe from the explosion. And if that were to happen, Veritalon would be drained and helpless. It's simple: Veritalon can let the universe and everything in it survive, including Luminous—but Veritalon would die. On the other hand, he can let the universe die, but he would live."

"Is Luminous really that insane to make that kind of gamble?" asked Tal.

"Afraid so. But that's the bad news. I managed to sneak in and steal the orbs. With their power, we can disarm Luminous's little toy."

"Why didn't you bring the orbs with you?" inquired Siegfried.

"Something else is going on—or someone else is involved. When I recovered the orb of death, Luminous seemed to know exactly where I was. I didn't want to run that risk again, so I hid them. But we're running out of time. Once Facade wakes up, she'll use her powers to find the orbs no matter where they are. Come on, move it or lose it—literally."

Aerial turned to Siegfried. "You're not seriously thinking of trusting him, are you? It's because of him all this happened in the first place!"

Siegfried thought for a bit and then replied, "If what he says is true, Veritalon and the rest of the universe is in danger. Besides, if he was in league with Luminous, she'd already be here. We have to trust him."

"Fine!" Aerial turned to Rilic. "But Luminous isn't our only problem. I'll be keeping an eye on you!"

"Oh, don't flirt."

Aerial was not the least bit amused.

Tal once again held Huiliang close, and the entire group shot into the air, following Rilic and heading for the United States.

— CHAPTER FOUR —

The Four Warriors of the Apocalypse

DOCTOR SMITH AND LUCIA WORKED diligently to repair the damaged photon battery, but it seemed luck was not on their side.

President Landgard entered the room. "How are things coming?"

"Not good," reported Smith grimly. "A lot of the vital parts have been damaged. It is possible we might be able to get it running, but at this point we need a miracle."

"Well, you two keep at it. Right now that machine is the only prayer we have."

Victor Landgard left the room. Lucia and Doctor

Smith looked at each other, knowing they had their work cut out for them.

After walking some distance, James Staten finally found a vehicle that looked intact: a large yellow school bus. James didn't like the idea of leaving the area in such a large target, but he knew walking on foot was probably worse. After climbing inside the bus, he turned over the engine, and it started right up. James put his foot on the gas and left the area as fast as the bus could go.

Inside the Spirex, Luminous began to smile as the crystal that hovered between the four warriors began to glow brightly. Finally all four warriors—Facade, Inferno, Rampage, and Vartile—opened their eyes.

"It is finished," said the emotionless Facade.

Luminous walked up to them. "Excellent. But unfortunately we have no time to celebrate. Veritalon will be here any time now, and the orbs have been stolen."

Inferno was infuriated. "You swore! You promised us victory!"

"Calm yourself, Inferno! All we have to do is find one orb before Veritalon arrives." With that, Luminous turned to Facade. "Can you find them?"

"If they are still on this world, yes."

"Oh, they're still here. I'll bet my future on it."

Facade closed her eyes. "Yes, I see them. They're not far from this place."

"Good." Luminous took the crystal in her hand. "Come. We have no time to lose."

All five left the Spirex, heading for the orbs.

James Staten slammed on the brakes just in time to avoid hitting a little girl who walked down the center of the street. Anna saw the bus heading for her, but she was too overcome with shock to care. Suddenly a soldier came out of the bus.

James knelt down. "Are you all right?" Anna said nothing; all she had was a blank, soulless look on her face. "Where're your parents?" Still nothing.

James quickly scooped up little Anna in his arms. He put her in the bus and could tell she was severely deprived of food. James gave her some of his military rations. Anna was so hungry that she practically swallowed the food without chewing.

After sitting little Anna down in one of the seats, he said, "Now, you stay right there. I'm getting you out of here." James once again took the wheel of the bus and continued down the road.

Just a few miles away, Rilic took Siegfried, Tal, Huiliang, and Aerial to where he had hidden the orbs. Siegfried knew they probably didn't have much time. "Okay, we have to—"

Siegfried didn't even get to finish the sentence before Luminous, Facade, Inferno, Rampage, and Vartile arrived.

"Get behind me, Huiliang!" said Tal. Huiliang did so instantly.

Luminous instantly asserted her position as leader. "Well, Rilic, I was really quite distressed when I heard you'd stolen my orbs, but now it seems I should be thanking you. Not only did you retrieve all the orbs in a nice little package, but you gathered together all of Veritalon's scouts for me to kill. I would like to thank you, but you'll understand if I don't."

Rilic glared at her with a look that could kill. "Go to hell!"

Luminous smiled. "Well, one of us is going there." She addressed the four warriors. "Kill them all. Bring the orbs to me."

Everyone sprang into action.

"Split up!" ordered Siegfried.

Rilic fought Vartile. Siegfried battled Rampage. Tal took on Inferno. Aerial dealt with Facade. The only spectators were Luminous on one side of the field and Huiliang, who was standing next to the orbs.

Rilic ran toward Vartile, his right demon arm stretched out, hoping to impale the creature on his claws. But within microseconds of hitting him, Vartile simply disappeared. Rilic's eyes open wide as he looked around; Vartile was nowhere to be seen. Then far behind him, Rilic could hear Vartile laughing.

"Ha! You move like a slug," Vartile said.

Rilic once again ran toward Vartile with the same results. Suddenly Rilic crumpled to the ground, bleeding. Vartile's giant claws had cut a hole in his belly.

Vartile licked the blood from his claws. "I'm going to carve you up like beef."

Rampage charged toward Siegfried like a battering ram. Siegfried managed to block the blow, but the force of it sent him flying through several neighborhoods. Siegfried tried desperately to recover as he struggled to his feet. His vision was spinning.

Inferno walked toward Tal, her fingers outstretched as flames of fire came out of the tips. All Tal could do was back away from the wall of flames with which Inferno hounded him.

"What's the matter, boy? Am I too hot for you?"

Tal knew the only way to win was to get on the inside, but getting close to Inferno was like getting near a towering volcano.

Aerial immediately went in to action. She knew she had to act quickly before Facade pulled one of her tricks. After rushing headlong into battle, Aerial flew straight for Facade. Upon impact, Aerial passed straight through Facade's body like a hologram. Aerial was stunned for a moment but quickly realized that the hologram couldn't possibly be Facade. She turned her attention away from it and looked for the real Facade. Then suddenly and unexpectedly, the hologram hit Aerial in the back with an energy blast. Now Aerial was more confused than ever. *Holograms can't produce energy!* she thought to herself.

But the worst was yet to come. The single Facade immediately split into four and surrounded Aerial. Aerial knew the only way to get out of this was to go to the one place where she had the advantage: the sky. Aerial immediately tried to ascend, but something dragged her back down, sending her crashing to the ground.

The four Facades created an energy net, preventing Aerial from flying and trapping her within. Aerial screamed in pain. The four Facades electrified the net, killing Aerial slowly.

Siegfried staggered toward Rampage. Rampage did not charge; right now he had other things on his mind. *This is pathetic!* he thought to himself. *Luminous promised me a true fight, and all I get is this? I might as well be fighting a child!* Rampage looked around at Rilic, Tal, and Aerial. "May be if I took on all four of them at once?" But after seeing how much fun the other warriors were having, he knew they wouldn't stand for that. "This sucks!" he finally said out loud. Nobody paid attention to a word he said.

General Nathan Staten reported, "Mr. President, we've got a satellite trained on some kind of battle going on just outside of Washington."

"Let's see it," said Victor. Immediately the satellite gave them a bird's-eye view of the battle. Victor was puzzled.

"I don't understand it. They're fighting among themselves again. Why would they do that?"

General Staten interjected. "We thought we were in the middle of an invasion, but maybe we're in the middle of a war."

Just then President Landgard noticed Huiliang. "There. Who's that? Zoom in."

The soldier running the equipment complied instantly.

"She's human," said a surprised Victor. "I need to know who she is right away!"

At that moment Luminous's attention strayed from the battle and rested on Huiliang. Luminous talked to herself. "I might as well finish her off now; it'll save time." Luminous began to walk toward Huiliang.

Huiliang didn't even notice. Her attention was fixed on Tal's battle with Inferno.

Tal was still dodging the lethal onslaughts of Inferno's flames. Then he noticed out of the corner of his eye Luminous heading for Huiliang. "No!" he shouted. Fearing for Huiliang's life, he flew straight into the wall of flames and came out the other end, right in front of Inferno.

For the first time in her life, Inferno was surprised and a little afraid.

Tal gave her a right hook, sending her flying. Then he turned back and headed straight for Luminous.

Luminous was only seconds from stretching out her hand and taking Huiliang's life, but she noticed Tal racing toward her. A surprised Luminous didn't know what to make of this and decided to fall back.

Everything happened so fast that Huiliang didn't even notice her own life was in danger until she saw Tal flying toward her and Luminous withdrawing.

The commotion captured Facade's attention, who was still electrocuting Aerial. For that one brief moment her attention was on Tal and not on Aerial.

Aerial saw her chance and took it. Immediately Aerial grabbed the energy net and poured all of her power into it. The energy caused a feedback. All that the four Facades saw when they looked back was a massive energy surge.

Aerial drew in a deep breath of relief. Facade was gone. However, Aerial was so drained and weak that she couldn't even make it to her feet.

Tal asked Huiliang with deep concern, "Are you all right?"

Huiliang shook her head, realizing that she was only seconds from death.

Suddenly Tal screamed, "Get behind me!"

A massive funnel of flames engulfed Tal and Huiliang. Tal managed to create a barrier that protected him and Huiliang, but his body was already past its limits; he was running on sheer willpower.

Inferno was more furious than ever. "No one does that to me!" she screamed, relentlessly keeping up her onslaught.

Suddenly the sky burst into brilliant light. Thunder and lightning seemed to come from everywhere. Everyone on the planet stood, amazed.

"What in god's name?" said President Victor Landgard, his eyes open wide.

While looking at the bright sky, the Australian shaman proclaimed, "He is among us now."

James Staten stopped the bus as his eyes just about popped out. "Holy shit!"

For the first time since her parents had died, little Anna's face expressed the emotion of wonder. She put her little hand on the window of the bus and felt the warmth of the light.

Inferno, Rampage, and Vartile were no longer attacking; rather, they seemed afraid. Only Luminous was confident and unflinching.

"He's here!" said Rilic confidently.

Inferno, Rampage, and Vartile retreated back to where Luminous stood as Veritalon descended.

Huiliang couldn't even look directly at the new arrival; it was like looking directly into the sun.

Aerial, Tal, Siegfried, and Rilic healed due to being in his presence. Within a few seconds they were completely restored.

Veritalon spoke with a voice that resonated power. He turned to Aerial, Tal, Siegfried, and Rilic, and he smiled. "Well done, all of you. I have never been more proud to be your father."

Aerial was full of concern. "Father, Luminous is planning to—"

"I already know, daughter," he addressed all of them. "But now is not the time. You must take the orbs and the human child and leave this place immediately. I will confront Luminous. Now, go quickly."

They bowed and flew off, taking all eight orbs and Huiliang with them.

Veritalon stood to face Luminous, Inferno, Rampage, and Vartile alone.

"It's about time you showed up, old man!" exclaimed Luminous.

"Luminous, don't do this. You were one of my greatest creations. Please, daughter, don't do this."

But Luminous didn't want to hear any of it; all she felt was hatred. "Shut up!" She pulled out the crystal. "I have waited for this day for a long time! Now you will finally bow to *me*, or forfeit everything you've made!

"Neither I nor the ones who follow me will ever bow to you."

"Fine, then. What happens next is on your head. Will you sacrifice yourself to save them, or are you just a coward? All this because you weren't willing to do one simple little thing. You are truly pathetic."

Luminous released the crystal into the air. As she predicted, Veritalon created a barrier around it, shielding the universe from its detonation. Veritalon dropped to the ground. Luminous walked over to him, smiling. "Not so tough now, are you? I bet now you're wishing you'd bowed."

Luminous kicked him in the side, opening him with a gushing wound. Luminous knelt down. "I think it's time we end this!" With that, Luminous dug her nails into Veritalon's chest and ripped out his heart. Veritalon was dead. Inferno, Rampage, and Vartile roared in victory; their long-awaited revenge had finally come. Luminous looked up to the sky, still holding Veritalon's heart. "Now the universe has a new god—me!"

Inside the bunker, President Landgard and General Staten could see everything, although they couldn't make out the words.

"What just happened down there?" asked General Staten.

Victor replied, "I think the wrong side just one."

All over the world, lights from space refused to shine, as if light itself refused to visit earth. The sun, moon, and stars were invisible, drowning the planet in a sea of darkness. The only lights that remained were the ones produced by man.

After looking up at the sky and seeing no stars, the shaman began to cry. "He is gone."

James Staten nearly ran the yellow bus off the road. One minute the sky was filled with light, and the next there was complete and utter darkness. James turned on the headlights and looked up at the sky. "Okay, that can't be good!"

Little Anna curled back in her seat, more afraid than ever.

Rilic fell to the ground, his eyes full of tears. "What have I done?"

Aerial almost attacked Rilic, but Siegfried held her back. She spat, "I knew we couldn't trust you! This is all your fault! If it wasn't for you, Luminous would of never have found this planet!"

"That's enough, Aerial," said Siegfried.

"But this is all his fault!"

Siegfried looked at her with tears in his eyes. "We're all hurting."

Aerial knelt down and began to sob bitterly.

Despite the lack of light, Huiliang could still see the light of her protectors. She didn't quite know what was going on, but she knew Tal was in pain. She lovingly and gently put her hand on his back and asked, "What's wrong?"

Tal, looked at her with a heavy heart. "Veritalon's dead. Luminous murdered him."

Huiliang embraced Tal, trying to comfort him. The two of them wept together.

After an hour of darkness, the sun, stars, and moon began to shine again, but perhaps a little less bright.

The CIA finally recovered the information on Huiliang. Soon General Staten had a ton of material to show Victor. "Her name is Huiliang. Father and mother deceased. Apparently she has been living with her uncle, General Vang Kai, in the city of Beijing. From what our resources can tell us, General Vang Kai was in charge of Project Black Dragon, a top-secret Chinese lab. We suspect this is where the Chinese were keeping their orb."

"Okay, so how does a nice little Chinese girl end up with protectors like them?"

"No idea, sir."

"I want you to get in touch with the Chinese government. We need to find her."

"Already tried, sir. They assumed she died in Beijing."

"Well, I need you to find either her or one of her alien friends. If Alain and Lucia are unable to get that battery fixed, they might be our only option."

"Yes, sir."

Siegfried addressed the group. "All right, we need to get going."

Everyone had lost the will to go on, especially Rilic. "Go? Go where? Veritalon is dead. Luminous and three of the four warriors are still out there, and only Veritalon and Luminous know how to use the orbs! Oh, and I almost forgot: it is only a matter of time before Luminous tears this planet apart to find us! Have I left anything out?"

"Yeah, you did. We met a shaman who has the sight."

"You're kidding."

Aerial chimed in, a smile on her face. "That's right! If that shaman can use the orbs or knows somebody who can, we can stop this from ever happening!"

Everyone's spirits were raised, especially Rilic's, due to the hope of redemption. "Well, what's everyone standing around here for? We need to get going!"

– CHAPTER FIVE –

The Yellow School Bus

LUMINOUS, INFERNO, RAMPAGE, AND VARTILE returned to the Spirex. Luminous still possessed Veritalon's heart. As she looked at it in the palm of her hand, she began to smile. "Well, I may have lost a crystal, but at least I have a heart."

"What are we doing back here?" demanded Inferno. "We should be looking for those orbs!"

Vartile added, "But with Facade dead, we have no way of finding them. They could be anywhere on this dirt heap."

Luminous was very calm and collective. "Don't worry, my friends. We will find them easily enough."

"How?" asked Rampage.

"We'll deal with that later. Right now, we have to free the rest of our comrades."

"How is that possible?" inquired Vartile. "Only Veritalon has the power to open the rift."

Luminous set Veritalon's heart on a pedestal. "And he will. It is simply a matter of the heart." With that Luminous shot a bolt of energy straight at Veritalon's heart. The heart acted like a prism, opening the rift. Suddenly billions of ruthless demonic warriors began to emerge. "Welcome to earth, my warriors. I believe you will enjoy your stay."

Every warrior cried out, "Long live Luminous!"

Luminous drank in their worship for a bit, but then she decided it was time to get back to business. After stretching out her hand and creating a holographic projection of Rilic, Tal, Siegfried, Aerial, and Huiliang, she announced to everyone, "These fugitives have my orbs. Go track them down, and when you find them, report their position back to me."

Every warrior proclaimed, "Yes, almighty Luminous."

Outside the Spirex, every warrior spread out from the area, searching for the orbs.

"Excellent," said Vartile. "It shouldn't take them long to track those pathetic weaklings down."

Luminous knew better. "No, those warriors I just sent out are merely a distraction. We'll use the humans to find them. Fear—I love it."

Aerial's eagle eyes saw the swarm of warriors far off. "If we try to fly away, those things are bound to spot us."

Siegfried agreed. "Then we'll have to find another way."

Just then Aerial spotted a yellow school bus proceeding out of the area and heading for their location. "Hang on." Aerial walked out into the middle of the road, her hand outstretched to signal the driver to stop.

James Staten saw the most beautiful being he had ever seen. "An angel!" he said aloud. As he stopped the bus, Aerial came alongside the door. James opened it.

She said, "I'm sorry, but we require transport in your machine."

Aerial, Tal, Huiliang, Siegfried, and Rilic boarded the yellow school bus with the orbs in their possession.

Siegfried looked very serious, not realizing how ironic it sounded. He told James, "Take us to your leader. We have to find a shaman with the ability to unlock the eight orbs of creation. The survival of your world hangs in the balance."

James nodded. "I'll do my best, Mr. ...?"

"Siegfried. And this is my brother, Tal. She is Aerial, warrior of the skies. The human girl is Huiliang. And the one with the arm is Rilic."

Rilac sarcastically added, "Please don't stare."

James continued to drive down the road as Siegfried filled him in on the situation.

Little Anna was astonished by the beings—except for Rilic, whose right demon arm and cold mask frightened her.

As the yellow school bus traveled down the road, Huiliang had an idea. She grabbed a backpack she found in the bus and suggested putting all the orbs in it. Everyone agreed and decided that Huiliang should be in charge of watching over them, just as everybody would watch over her.

Luminous landed at the World News Headquarters in New York. Immediately every news camera was on her.

President Landgard was speaking to one of his subordinates when General Staten got his attention. "Mr. President, I think you'd better take a look at this."

There on the television was Luminous. "People of earth. My name is Luminous, your new goddess and master. Among you are five fugitives. Their names are Rilic, Aerial, Tal, and Siegfried. They are accompanied by a Chinese girl named Huiliang. Anyone found harboring these fugitives will be killed on sight. However, anyone who reports their location to he or one of my soldiers will be rewarded beyond all physical measure. Stand by my side, and this planet will prosper. Stand against me, and this is your fate." Luminous raised her hand and wiped out half of New York City "Anyone who is listening to me and knows where they are, the fate of your world is in your hands." With that, Luminous left.

General Staten looked at President Landgard. "Well, sir?"

President Landgard remained strong. "We don't cooperate with terrorists, even if they are gods! But I want those five found!"

"Yes, sir."

While looking at little Anna, Rilic began to think back on what Veritalon had said. "Love her as a father should. Then and only then will you be fully restored." Rilic sat down next to Anna.

Anna was still afraid of him and moved over.

Rilic said, "Yeah, I don't blame you. I have that effect on people, especially little girls." Just then Rilic caught Anna staring at his right demon arm. "This isn't my original, but it's kind of grown on me—literally. So, what's your name?" Anna remained silent. "Oh, come on. You have to have a name. Or are you nameless?"

Anna still remained silent.

Just then Rilic had an idea. Using his left hand, he materialized the most beautiful and largest diamond Anna had ever seen. "Do you like this?" Anna nodded. "Do you want this?" Anna nodded again out of excitement.

"Okay, we're going to play a little game called 'Repeat after Me.' The rules are simple: I say a word, and you repeat it. Technically you wouldn't really be talking to me—you'd just be repeating what I say. Are you ready?"

Anna nodded.

"Hippopotamus."

Anna answered in the most beautiful little voice he'd ever heard. "Hippopotamus."

"Rhinoceros."

"Rhinoceros," she parroted.

"Wrong."

Little Anna was confused. "Why?"

"No, not why. I said 'wrong.' You lose." Rilic started to put the diamond away. Anna began to cry. "Oh, that's my weak spot: girls crying. I didn't think you'd be a sore loser. Here." Rilic handed the diamond to Anna, who cheered right up. For the first time since her parents died, she smiled.

James looked at the gas gauge: the yellow school bus was running on empty. Finally he noticed a gas station. He realized that the chances of finding gasoline in this place was slim, because of the looters. Still, he was out of options and knew there might be a small chance.

"Why are we stopping?" asked Aerial.

"We're running out of gas."

"What's gas?" asked Siegfried.

"It's what this machine runs on."

James pulled in. Everyone got off; the yellow school bus was not the only thing that was running on empty. James, Anna, and Huiliang were getting very hungry, and James had no more army rations left. The group entered the gas station, a privately owned truck stop.

As everybody started looking around, James felt the cold end of a shotgun pointed at the back of his head. A voice came from behind him. "You have no right to force your way in here. This is my place."

No sooner did the man finish his sentence than James could no longer feel the end of the shotgun against his head. James turned around. There in front of him stood a forty-year-old man holding a shotgun.

The man was no longer pointing the gun at James; the barrel rested on the floor. The old gentleman seemed more concerned about Rilic, Aerial, and the sons of thunder.

The man's eyes were open wide as he said, "It's you! It's all of you! Thank god you're here! Thank god you're all here!"

"You know us?" asked Aerial.

"By reputation, yes."

Because she didn't understand English, Huiliang asked Tal, "What's happening?"

"He knows us somehow. The question is, how?"

"How do you know us?" asked a suspicious Rilic.

The old man stalled. "Oh, that's not important. The important thing is that you are here right now. What can I do for all of you?"

James spoke up. "We need gas, food, and supplies."

"Of course, of course! I've got plenty of food around! Fortunately I've been able to keep the scavengers away. Please, help yourself. I'll go and fill up your bus!" With that the excited old man walked out of the building.

James, Anna, and Huiliang ate as much as they could and took as much as they could carry.

James couldn't help but notice that Aerial, Rilic, and the sons of thunder didn't eat a bite. James asked Aerial, "Is something wrong? You haven't eaten anything."

"Our nutritional requirements are quite different from yours. For example, we don't need to eat"

"Well, that's convenient. You must save a lot of money on groceries."

Aerial gave off a beautiful smile and a laugh at that remark.

Upon seeing this, Rilic thought back to what Veritalon had told him, "And know this: for what you have done, you shall never have Aerial's heart again. She shall give it to one more worthy than you."

Not very far away, Rampage was on the hunt. Suddenly one of Luminous's hideous scouts came flying up to him. "My Lord Rampage, we have them. An earth man reported their location." It pointed westward. "Just a few miles in that direction. The human reported we would recognize the location by a large yellow vehicle."

Rampage grinded his teeth together in anticipation. "Excellent!"

"I will return to the Spirex and inform Luminous."

But before the scout could leave, Rampage grabbed him and twisted his head off from his body. The body fell to the ground. Rampage still held the head in his giant hand and replied, "That won't be necessary. I will inform Luminous myself—after I'm done with them, that is." With that, Rampage dropped the head and let it fall to the ground. "Finally—some real action!"

Back at the gas station, the old man finally returned.

"It takes you that long to pump gas?" asked Rilic.

"Oh, sorry! I had some errands to run."

James interjected. "Well, we'd better get out of here. Thank you for your cooperation."

The old man continued to stall. "Wait! Can't you stay

a little longer? Everyone's gone now, and it's been a while since I've spoken with anyone!"

"I'm sorry, but we really need to go."

"Wait!"

Just then everyone heard a huge crash outside, like a huge boulder dropped from a forty-story building. Everybody rushed outside. There stood Rampage.

"How did he find us?" asked Aerial.

Rilic looked back at the old man and replied, "I can take a guess."

James grabbed the old man by the shirt. "You told them where we are?"

"I had to! It's the only way to save us! Can't you see that?"

"What the hell have you done!"

Rampage had heard enough. "Shut up! I came here for a fight, not to watch you insects chatter!"

James let the old man go. The man ran off into the distance.

Rilic commented, "That's weird—only Rampage is here. I don't see Luminous or the others anywhere."

"Oh, don't worry," said Rampage. "I've made sure no one will interrupt us."

Aerial commented, "You can't be serious. Even you can't take on all of us."

"You underestimate my power! I'll take you all on one at a time or all together—it makes no difference to me."

Siegfried said to his warriors, "Okay, Tal, you take the left flank. I'll take the right. Rilic, your demon arm may be the only thing strong enough to take him on; you'll go in from the front. Aerial, you'll attack from the sky. James, you'll look after Anna and Huiliang. Let's go!"

The fight was on. Rilic, Siegfried, and Tal charged for Rampage. Rampage pounded his enormous fists against the ground, creating a shockwave and sending Siegfried and Tal reeling backward. Rilic managed to avoid the shockwave—only to have Rampage's fist send him flying as well.

Tal turned to Siegfried. "I think we may have underestimated this guy!"

"Yeah, he's a lot stronger than he looks."

Rilic got back up. "I sure am getting tired of being outclassed!"

Rampage was disappointed. "Is this all you pathetic warriors can offer me?"

The three of them continued the assault on Rampage. The sons of thunder proved to be quite the tag-team. When Rampage's attention was drawn to one of them, the other one would turn up the heat. Rilic's right demon arm acted like a shield against Rampage, and yet it was still like fighting a mountain of strength.

Aerial could barely see the battle in the distance as she flew. While looking back, she said to herself, "Okay, this should be far enough." Then she started flying toward the battlefield. Her speed continued to accelerate exponentially. As her speed increased, a supersonic shockwave formed in front of her.

Back at the battlefield, the sons of thunder and Rilic continued their attack until Siegfried shouted, "Get down!" Everyone except for Rampage dove for the ground.

Aerial hit Rampage with so much force that the monster experienced pain for the first time; one of his horns broke off and fell to the ground. Aerial was completely exhausted. Although she had hit Rampage with tremendous force, his rock-hard body did a number on her as well.

Rampage was wounded, but his rage spelled certain doom for Aerial. As he moved toward her, his eyes were full of hate. "You're going to pay for that! You'll pay for it!"

Suddenly James Staten jumped on Rampage's back. Rampage tried to grab him, but he was so large he couldn't quite reach James. "Get off me, you little maggot!" Unexpectedly, the invincible Rampage cried out in pain and torment. For one brief moment, everyone was astonished. What kind of powers had this ordinary human soldier achieved to cause Rampage so much agony? The answer to that became apparent when they saw what kind of weapon he was holding in his hand: it was Rampage's own horn. James had picked it up and was now stabbing Rampage in the back, deeper and deeper.

"Now is our chance!" shouted Siegfried.

Rilic and the sons of thunder immediately renewed their assault on the monstrous Rampage.

Rampage was no longer having fun. After taking the lives of many others, he was now fighting for his own life. Out of pure desperation, with one below he hit Rilic and the sons of thunder aside. "Get off me! Get off me!" Rampage screamed.

The young marine would not give up and continued the assault. He said, "For God and country, I will end you!"

Finally the monster Rampage fell to the ground dead.

Rilic and the sons of thunder looked at James, surprised.

After putting the horn in his pocket, James simply said, "You guys were moving a little slow for me."

All of them gave a surprising chuckle.

James walked over to Aerial and helped her up. "Are you all right?"

Aerial nodded. Her eyes gave off the glow of when she saw the man that she would love for the first time.

Despite having no powers and merely being a human, this American soldier had brought down one of the strongest warriors in the universe.

"All right, people," said Rilic. "Two down; three to go. Let's move out."

The group jumped back in the yellow school bus. Siegfried started it right up. Surprisingly, the old man really had filled the tank.

"That's odd," remarked Tal.

Rilic simply said, "He was probably just worried that we were watching him."

"Mr. President," reported General Staten, "there has been another incident."

President Landgard sighed. "Don't tell me; let me guess. We're one step behind them."

"I'm afraid so, sir."

President Landgard looked up at the screen. On it was a satellite picture of Rampage's dead body.

"Looks like you're right, General. It was definitely them. Where did they go next?"

"According to our intelligence, they're heading west. That means the next town in their path is Charleston."

"I want a team deployed immediately. But keep it low-key; we don't want our enemies to know we've joined forces."

"Right away, sir."

At that moment, Luminous had a burst of rage and destroyed three of her own soldiers.

Not knowing what was bothering her, Vartile asked, "What's wrong, my queen?"

"Rampage is dead! He must have tried to fight them all himself. That damned fool! Why am I surrounded by fools? At this rate we'll all be killed off by weaklings!" She turned to Inferno and Vartile. "Let me make this quite clear: if either of you two find them, don't engage. Contact me! Is there any part of that statement you two did not understand?"

Vartile and Inferno shook their heads.

"Good!" Luminous sat back on her throne and began to think. *If they miraculously find someone who knows how to use the orbs, all this will be for nothing. In case this thing goes south, I'll need insurance. Time for plan B.*

Lucia and Doctor Smith were still trying to get the photon battery to work. Then, to Doctor Smith's surprise, Lucia got it working.

"How did you do that?" he asked her.

Lucia smiled. "I'm a prodigy, remember? Come on. We have to get this to Victor."

Miles away, the dead body of Veritalon lay quiet. Then his fingers began to twitch. His body and his heart were being restored.

Doctor Smith and Lucia entered into the main control room. Doctor Smith went first. "Mr. President, we got it working, sir."

"Good work, Doctor."

"Oh, don't thank me, sir. It was Lucia."

"Good work, Lucia."

Lucia smiled. "Thank you, sir."

Victor Landgard turned to General Staten. "I want that weapon loaded on an F-18 immediately."

"Yes, sir. What's the target?"

"That crystal structure. We're going to take it out."

The yellow school bus finally arrived in Charleston. Although it had been days since the first attack on Washington, everyone in the city was paranoid and on edge. Riot police walked up and down the streets.

"Luminous probably has the entire planet looking for us," said Tal.

Siegfried nodded. "Which means we're probably going to have to travel in disguise."

"Oh, no," remarked Rilic. "Not that stupid kids game, Fool Me."

"Do you have any other options?"

"Fine."

Huiliang turned to Tal. "Fool Me?"

"It's a game we used to play when we were children. Kind of like our version of hide-and-seek, except for the fact that we hide in plain sight. We take on the form of the planet's inhabitants, and then we try to guess which ones are the true inhabitants and which ones are not."

Rilic felt that playing such a childish game was beneath him, but he had no choice. "All right, let's get this over with."

Rilic, Aerial, and the sons of thunder concentrated for a bit and then assumed human appearances. Every single one of them looked as attractive as they did before, except this time they looked human.

The entire group exited the yellow school bus and joined the crowds on the streets. As they walked along, James addressed all of them. "I just need to find a pay phone or something I can use to contact my father. He's a general in the marines."

Just then Rilic noticed something. "Don't look now, but I think we're being followed."

Siegfried noticed it too. "You're right. Let's go down that alley and see what he wants."

The group immediately turned right; the mysterious man followed. Suddenly Rilic grabbed the man and pinned him up against the wall of the alley. "Why are you following us?"

"Ow! Damn, you're strong!"

James could hardly believe it and recognized that voice. "Stumpy!"

"Hey, ugly American. Who're your friends?" He looked at Aerial and Huiliang. "And who are they? Damn, man, how do you get so lucky?"

"It's a long story. Can you get me in touch with the general?"

"Sure, as soon as your friend lets me down."

Rilic released him. "Sorry."

"That's all right. I've had worse."

"Oh, I wouldn't brag about that, if I were you."

As the group headed toward Stumpy's military Jeep, he filled them in. "The president sent me to find you guys. He witnessed some of your battles by satellite. I have to admit, you look different from what they told me." He turned to James. "Got to admit, I didn't expect to find you with them."

"Yeah I kind of ran into them. Like I said, long story." James picked up the microphone in the military Jeep. "This is an emergency POTUS contact. Repeat, this is an emergency POTUS contact."

The soldier handling the com got President Landgard, General Staten, Lucia, and Doctor Smith's attention. "We have an emergency POTUS contact from Captain James Staten."

General Nathan Staten was relieved at the news his son was alive, but he knew the danger was not yet over. He picked up the mic and said, "Good to hear you're alive, boy."

"Thank you, sir." James Staten gave them his exact coordinates.

President Landgard gave the order. "I want them to be extracted and brought here ASAP."

Inside the Spirex, Luminous burst out laughing. "Now we have them!" Luminous, Inferno, and Vartile began heading toward Charleston.

"Well, I guess all we can do now is wait," said James.

Just then Luminous, Inferno, and Vartile arrived. Everyone had a look of astonishment and fear. Luminous was smiling. "Well, we meet again. Did all of you really think you could get away from me?"

Rilic was more pissed off than ever. "How do you keep finding us, you bitch?"

"God. That being said, I have more resources then you can possibly imagine. Anyway, it's been a merry chase, but now it's over. Time to die."

Everyone braced themselves for the battle, yet everyone knew that they would not survive this one.

Suddenly the earth began to shake, and light engulfed the sky. The universe itself seemed to roar.

"No!" screamed Luminous. "No! It can't be! It's impossible!"

"He's alive!" said Aerial, smiling with tears of joy in her eyes. "He's really alive!"

Rilic turned to Luminous. "Is it just me, or are you getting that feeling of déjà vu all over again?"

Little Anna began to smile out of wonder, as did everyone else in the group.

Stumpy's jaw dropped so wide it almost hit the ground. "No way!"

President Landgard's eyes opened widely, as did everyone else's in the room. "Here we go again!"

The shaman began to smile from ear to ear. "He has risen!"

Out of fear, all of Luminous's forces began to retreat back into their prison universe.

"No, no! Get back here!" demanded Luminous. No one paid attention, and they all ran away.

Rilic commented, "Like rats deserting a sinking ship."

The only ones who remained by Luminous's side were Inferno and Vartile. They were once again face-to-face with Veritalon himself.

Veritalon turned to Aerial, Rilic, and the sons of thunder. "Well done. Once again you four have proven yourself. Now, this is my battle to finish. Go. I will join you shortly."

With that, the group moved to a safer location to watch the battle.

Luminous was sick with hate. "Why can't you just stay dead? How did you come back?"

"Who created life and death?"

"Damn you!" Luminous turned to Inferno and Vartile. "We killed him once! We can do it again!"

Vartile used his great speed to slice a hole in Veritalon's belly—or at least he thought he did. Veritalon didn't seem to be injured at all, and yet there was some glowing liquid on Vartile's claws. Suddenly the liquid began to burn. It consumed Vartile's entire body until there was nothing left but smoke and ash.

Inferno was so afraid that she backed up. Unfortunately for her, Luminous was behind her. "Coward!" screamed Luminous as she ran her hand through Inferno's heart.

Now there was nobody left but Veritalon and Luminous.

"Fine!" exclaimed Luminous. "I'll kill you myself." With that, Luminous dislocated her jaw. She began to peel her lips and flesh away like a snake shedding its skin. Out of her mouth came the head of a great red dragon. Its wings came next, followed by its entire body. The dragon grew in size and strength, and it roared at Veritalon.

Veritalon simply held his hands up high and outstretched as he looked toward the sky and closed his eyes. Suddenly a brilliant burst of light hit him and engulfed his entire body. He also grew in size and strength as he changed into a great golden lion. The dragon and the lion launched for each other. Thunder ripped the sky in response to the horrific clash of the spiritual forces.

"My God!" said Victor, watching everything by satellite.

The com officer caught his attention. "Sir, the F-18 is approaching the crystal structure.

Victor was so wrapped up in the battle that he simply said, "Uh yeah. Uh, fire."

"You are clear to fire on target, Loner."

"Roger that," said the F-18 pilot. He fired the photon battery at the Spirex. Upon impact, the Spirex exploded into billions of pieces until nothing remained. Everyone in the presidential bunker cheered.

The Dragon blew fire at the lion, which countered with a roar that split the fire down the middle. Finally the lion bit the dragon in the neck. The dragon began to burn up from the inside until nothing was left. Luminous, the dark angel of light, was gone.

Everyone in the group could hardly believe it. "We won!" exclaimed Aerial. "We actually won!"

Veritalon returned to his normal form. With his hands outstretched, he restored to life everyone that was killed by Luminous and her followers. Washington DC, China, Ottawa, Brasilia, Buenos Aires, Moscow, and New York were restored as if nothing had happened.

General Vang Kai woke up in the top-secret Chinese laboratory. The last thing he could remember was protecting his niece, Huiliang. Now he was dazed and confused. *What happened?* he thought to himself.

Sergeant Nathan Johnson woke up in the center of Washington. The last thing he remembered was heading out of the city with the photon battery, but now the city was completely restored. "What the hell? I'm dead! Is this what happens when you die?" He looked around him. Other people seemed to be as confused as he was.

Veritalon walked up to the rest of the group. "Well done, all of you. You fought the good fight. And even though at times you felt like giving up, you did not give in. You have been faithful in the face of death. For that reason, I am now naming all of you guardians of earth."

"My Lord," said Aerial, "what about the orbs? Will you be taking them back to the eternal realm?"

"No. It is now up to humanity to decide what to do with that power. Enough power to lift mankind from the depths of hell and into heaven—or destroy them. Either way, they must choose their own course. Take the orbs back to their respective lands; their story is not yet written. Now, I must depart. Take good care of my creation." With a brilliant trail of light, Veritalon flew into space, becoming smaller and smaller until the group could no longer see him.

— CHAPTER SIX —
In Days to Come

I N WASHINGTON DC THE GOVERNMENT HELD A
ceremony. The president of the United States
commemorated Captain James Staten and Victor
Landgard for their courage and leadership. Aerial was
there in her beautiful human female disguise. General
Nathan Staten stood nearby. As the president pinned the
metal on Captain James Staten, Aerial smiled a beautiful
smile. General Nathan Staten had never been more proud
of his son. The president shook Victor Landgard's hand
as he presented him with a metal as well. Knowing that
Victor Landgard would no doubt when the election, the
president said, "It's good to know that this country's future
is in safe hands."

"Thank you, Mr. President."

"Not for long. That job belongs to you now."

After the ceremony, Aerial and James hopped into his convertible. James turned to her. "So what do you want to do first?"

"Well, if I'm going to be a guardian of earth, I have to know about it." She smiled as she said, "Show me your world." James smiled as well, and the two of them drove off together.

Rilic and Anna were at one of the largest theme parks in the world. Rilic was disguised as a human, and he smiled as he watched his adopted daughter on the carousel. Once again he began to think back on Veritalon's words: "Only she can redeem you." Although Rilic in his true form still had his right demon arm and deformed mouth, he knew now that was not what Veritalon meant. Anna redeemed his soul.

Just then a man walked up to him. "Hey."

"Hey," Rilic replied.

"Is that your daughter up there?"

Rilic smiled. "Yes, she is."

In Beijing, Tal landed just outside of General Vang Kai's house. He knocked on the door, and the general answered it. The two great soldiers bowed to each other, and then the general invited him in. Inside stood Huiliang, dressed in a beautiful Chinese kimono.

In New York City, night had fallen. Siegfried was on the top of the World Trade Center. While looking down at the beautiful lights of the city below, he became deeply concerned. "All those times. How? How did Luminous know where we were? No, it's not over—not yet. We're still missing something. But what?"

In the same city just a few miles away, a very rich man had dinner with a very attractive woman in his penthouse apartment. The man picked up a glass of champagne and handed it to the woman. He asked, "Are you sure that's what she wanted?"

"Luminous gave specific instructions that if her plan failed, that's what we are supposed to do."

The man raised his glass for a toast. "To revenge, then."

"To revenge."

In the vast Australian outback, the sun was rising. Everyone had left the shaman and gone back to their homes—except for one teenage boy. The boy turned to the shaman with a look of relief in his eyes. "It's over, isn't it? We are safe again!"

The shaman was not relieved at all. "No, I'm afraid not. More is coming. The night of the dragon has passed. Now the day of the beast begins."

The End—Or Just the Beginning ...

Printed in the United States
By Bookmasters